...dry was born in Lancaster and ...ves in Surrey with her husband and two children. She studied English at Manchester and Oxford and taught for some years in a variety of schools and colleges, including the University of Sierra Leone in West Africa. Cherith is now a full-time writer and has published science fiction novels for older children, plays, and short stories for both children and adults.

SURFERS

MUTINY IN SPACE

Cherith Baldry

Illustrated by
Mark Edwards

PUFFIN BOOKS

To Adam

PUFFIN BOOKS

Published by the Penguin Group
Penguin Books Ltd, 27 Wrights Lane, London W8 5TZ, England
Penguin Books USA Inc., 375 Hudson Street, New York, New York 10014, USA
Penguin Books Australia Ltd, Ringwood, Victoria, Australia
Penguin Books Canada Ltd, 10 Alcorn Avenue, Toronto, Ontario, Canada M4V 3B2
Penguin Books (NZ) Ltd, 182–190 Wairau Road, Auckland 10, New Zealand

Penguin Books Ltd, Registered Offices: Harmondsworth, Middlesex, England

First published 1997
3 5 7 9 10 8 6 4 2

Text copyright © Cherith Baldry, 1997
Illustrations copyright © Mark Edwards, 1997
All rights reserved

The moral right of the author and illustrator has been asserted

Filmset in Bembo

Made and printed in England by Clays Ltd, St Ives plc

British Library Cataloguing in Publication Data
A CIP catalogue record for this book is available from the British Library

ISBN 0-140-38489-8

Contents

Contents

Chapter One
The Trouble with Rivets

"3,561 . . . 3,562 . . ."

Jake Fraser crawled on hands and knees across the flight deck of the starship *Venture*, seething with fury. Above his head, lights flickered on display panels, and he could hear the faint hum of the ship's functions. Just below his nose, the deck plates were shiny enough to show him the blurred reflection of his own face and rumpled hair.

"3,563 . . ."

Jake squatted back on his heels, and stared at the command seat, as if he could let his anger stream out of his eyes and frizzle the sleek head that was all he could see of the seat's occupant. First Lieutenant Quentin. Clever, superior, cool, hateful Lieutenant Quentin. If it wasn't for Quentin, Jake thought, he wouldn't be stuck with this stupid, pointless job. When he remembered thinking in school that a space cadet's life would be exciting . . .

Exciting! Huh! He dropped back on to hands and knees.

"3,564 . . ."

He yelped as a boot jabbed him sharply in the ribs. Looking up he saw Cadet Ellie Carr, barely saving herself from falling over him.

"That hurt," he complained.

"Sorry," Ellie said. "I didn't see you down there. Have you lost something?"

"No."

"Then what are you doing?"

"Counting rivets."

Ellie stood looking down at him, a puzzled frown on her freckled face.

"Sorry," she said. "For a minute there I thought you said you were counting rivets."

"I *am* counting rivets," Jake said bitterly.

"Why?"

Jake's gaze swivelled again to the back of Lieutenant Quentin's head.

"I'm on report."

"Oh." Ellie's voice sounded as if she might be trying not to laugh. If she laughed, Jake thought, he would strangle her, report or no report. "What did you do?" Ellie asked.

"He says I was insubordinate," Jake said. "It was in that last emergency drill. I was getting into my suit and he said to me, 'Come on, lad; you're so slow you remind me of a Denebian swamp slug.' And I said, 'And you remind me of an Arcturan rock snake.'

4

So he put me on report."

"Oh dear." Ellie shook her head sympathetically. "That's bad. You should have said, 'You remind me of an Arcturan rock snake, *sir*.'"

Jake grunted. He knew he shouldn't have lost his temper. But it would never have happened if Captain Parry had been supervising the drill. Captain Parry never snapped. Captain Parry never made you feel as if you were too slow and too awkward, with about six thumbs. The unfairness of it boiled up inside Jake.

"And then," he said, "Quentin told me he wanted to know how many rivets there are in the entire *Venture*. And I've got to count 'em!"

This time Ellie let out a smothered sound. Her face had gone pink and her eyes were sparkling. Even her flame-red hair seemed to be springing out of its braid.

"You can laugh," Jake said, "but it's not funny. I know things about Mr High-and-Mighty Quentin that aren't funny at all."

"What things?" Ellie asked.

Jake sat back again and spoke in a lower voice. "I heard he spaced somebody."

Ellie stared at him. She was not laughing now. "Spaced somebody? Oh no . . . not even Quentin. I know he's tough, but –"

"He shoved somebody out of an

airlock," Jake said. "A tech in engineering. That's what I heard. For sloppy work. Quentin spaced him."

"I don't believe it," Ellie said. "He'd never get away with it. He'd be court martialled. They'd have to —"

She broke off as the command seat swivelled a half-turn and brought Lieutenant Quentin into full view. His cool gaze took in both cadets. He raised one brow.

"Short of a job, Cadet Carr?" he said silkily.

Ellie reddened.

"No, sir." Hastily she crossed the flight deck to Quentin's seat, nearly tripping over her own feet, and held out the electronic pad she was carrying. "Fuel consumption figures, sir."

Quentin took the pad and the light-pen, initialled the report, and handed them back. Without another word, he spun the chair away. Ellie went back to Jake, who was bent busily over his rivets again.

"3,565 . . ."

"D'you think he heard?" Ellie whispered.

"Nah. Better beat it, though. 3,566 . . ."

Ellie was turning to go when the flight-deck doors swished open and Mark Bowman appeared. Jake hissed annoyance. The third cadet on board the *Venture* was not one of his favourite people. Know-it-all, Jake thought. Quentin's pet. He even looked the part – all smart and shiny, hair trimmed to the exact regulation length, green cadet shirt pressed as if he'd just put it on. Jake felt just as scruffy as he knew he looked.

Mark had a black instrument like a fancy-looking camera slung over his shoulder. He pointed it at the Communications Officer, whose station was nearest the doors. The black object bleeped. Mark peered at its dials and made a note on his pad, then saluted crisply and moved on.

"What's he up to?" Jake muttered.

Mark's instrument was now bleeping at Lieutenant Quentin. Quentin looked up at him, brow raised once more.

"What's that, cadet?"

"Life-signs inspection, sir," Mark replied smartly. "Medical regulations, sir. You read out normal, sir."

"I'm delighted to hear it," Quentin drawled. "Next time, announce yourself before you point something at a combat officer. Or you might get a very nasty shock." He waved a hand, ignoring Mark's stammered apology. "Very well, cadet. Carry on."

Jake hid a grin. Maybe Mark was not so much Quentin's pet after all. He watched as Mark went up to Ellie and announced stiffly, "Life-signs inspection. Medical regs."

"Go right ahead," Ellie said.

The black box bleeped.

"You're so normal, you're weird," Mark said, checking his dials.

"Gee, thanks," said Ellie.

"Don't mention it." He pointed the instrument at Jake. The bleeps were louder and faster. "Hey, your stress levels are right up," Mark said. "Better watch it. You could go just like that." He snapped his fingers.

"I'll stuff that thing down your throat," Jake said, "and see what it does for your stress levels."

Mark looked injured.

"It's for your own good," he said. "Your health, safety and efficiency, and – hey," he added, "what are you doing down there?"

11

Jake did not answer.

"Counting rivets," Ellie said helpfully.

"Counting rivets? But what . . .?" A massive grin spread over Mark's face. "Hey, has Quentin got you on report? He has, hasn't he? Counting rivets, eh? How many are there, then?"

"Shove off, Bowman," Jake said through his teeth.

Mark's grin vanished. He examined Jake as he might have examined a splash of mud on his polished boot.

"Don't blame me," he said. "It's not my fault. I'll bet you said something you shouldn't, didn't you? It would be just like you, Fraser."

"Mind your own business."

"I wish you two would stop

bickering," Ellie said. "Give it a rest, can't you?"

"I'm not bickering," Mark said. He looked smug. "I know how to behave. Nobody puts me on report."

If you got to count all the rivets in the ship for cheeking an officer, what was the punishment for thumping a fellow cadet on the flight deck, Jake wondered. He was staring blankly at the deck plates, not wanting to find out, when a horrible thought struck him.

"Oh heck!" he said. "I've lost count!"

But before he had finished speaking, the flight-deck doors swished open again. Jake looked up and what he saw drove all thoughts of rivets out of his head.

Two security guards stood there, blocking the doorway. Even though they were the *Venture*'s own men, they looked very big and very dangerous. They each held a laser cannon, trained on the flight-deck crew.

Chapter Two
Mutiny!

ONE OF THE guards said, "Everybody hold it right there."

In the pause that followed, he saluted. "All secure, sir," he said.

"Thank you, sergeant," Lieutenant

Quentin said. "At ease."

He sounded completely unsurprised. Jake noticed that the rest of the officers on the flight deck, though they had stopped what they were doing to listen, did not look surprised either. Uneasily, he got to his feet.

Lieutenant Quentin glanced round and fixed his eyes on the three cadets.

"You," he said. He pointed to the patch of deck in front of him. "Here."

Slowly, exchanging looks with each other, they obeyed. They cautiously mounted the step that separated the command area from the rest of the flight deck, and stood with their backs to the guards holding the laser cannon;

Jake could almost feel the barrels boring into him.

"Now," Lieutenant Quentin said, when they were in position, "you may begin by addressing me as Captain Quentin."

"What?" Jake and Ellie exclaimed together.

"What do you mean?" Jake went on. "Why should we call you Captain Quentin? What have you done with Captain Parry?"

Quentin smiled. It was not a friendly smile. It reminded Jake of the cold, silent spaces between the stars.

"What do you think I've done?" he said.

Jake gaped. "You spaced the

17

captain?" he said. "Then it *was* true, about that tech!" Wildly, he swung round and spoke to the other officers at their stations. "You heard what he said! He spaced the captain! Aren't you going to do anything about it?"

There was no reply. Jake looked from one officer to the next, down the line of workstations. Communications, navigation, science, weapons. All four of them wore a copy of Quentin's small, cold smile.

"You all knew . . ." Jake said, and fell silent.

"This is mutiny," Ellie said.

Lieutenant Quentin steepled his fingers and looked at her over them.

"An ugly word," he said. "I prefer

'takeover'. To be honest," he went on, "service life bores me. I expect to find it more exciting – and rewarding – as an independent operator."

"You mean a pirate," Ellie said.

Quentin raised his brows at her.

"Another ugly word."

"I don't believe this!" Jake said, beginning to recover from the shock. "You would never get the crew – not all the crew – to follow you."

"True," Quentin said. "Not all of them. But enough."

"And the others?" Ellie asked.

"The others?" Quentin's smile returned. "Ah, yes, the others. I think you might find them with the captain."

His amusement faded. His face was

cold. When he spoke again, his voice had hardened.

"All I have to decide now is what to do with the three of you. I'm a reasonable man. I prefer to give you a choice. You may decide to join me. I can offer you good chances of promotion, especially now, with . . . vacancies in the command crew. If not, provided you co-operate, I will put you off the ship at our first suitable planetfall, and you can make your own way home. Your third choice is to give me trouble. I would not recommend it."

He was waiting for an answer. Jake and Ellie looked at each other. Jake could see his own dismay reflected in Ellie's face.

"Well?"

Quentin snapped out the word, speaking directly to Mark. All the while, he had stood silent, eyes fixed on his medical monitor. Now he looked up. Jake could not understand his expression. He had that unbearable smug look again.

"Oh, I'll co-operate, sir," he said. "I don't want to be a hero. Especially a dead hero."

"Sensible," Quentin said.

Jake swallowed his disgust. He might have known that Mark would give in. Lick Quentin's boots just like that, without even trying to do anything! And looking so pleased about it too, as if it didn't matter that all those crew members were dead.

Inside his own mind, Jake was thinking frantically, wondering if there was anything he could do to fight Quentin. The first thing would be to stay free, to get off the flight deck. But every plan was stopped before it started by those two security guards with their laser cannon.

"And you, Cadet Carr?" Quentin was asking. "Are you going to be sensible too?"

Ellie took a step back. She put up her hands to cover her mouth. A whimpering sound came from her.

"Oh, sir, don't space me," she said. "I won't give any trouble, I promise."

Jake stared at her. This wasn't like

Ellie. She'd come through first year training somewhere near the top of the list. This was no time for her to start losing her cool, for goodness' sake!

"Cadet Carr —" Quentin began impatiently.

Ellie backed further away from him, beginning to sob. At the top of the step she lost her balance. Her arms windmilled frantically, and Jake caught a glimpse of her face with an almost comical expression of surprise as she fell backwards and crashed to the deck. She lay still.

"Unnecessary," Quentin said. He touched a button on the arm of his chair and spoke to his intercom. "Medical? Casualty on the flight deck.

Send two orderlies and an anti-grav stretcher."

While Quentin was speaking, Jake knelt down beside Ellie and checked her over. Her eyes were closed and she did not answer when he spoke to her, but she was breathing and he could not see any sign of obvious injury.

He got to his feet again, eyes shooting hatred at Quentin. More than anything he wanted Quentin scared, as he and Ellie were scared. Quentin with that stuck-up expression wiped off his face. It would be worth a lot to see that. One day, he promised himself silently, he would.

Quentin seemed content to wait for the medical team, and did not ask Jake for his decision. Jake was pleased to be ignored. He was starting to think again. Ellie's injury had hardened his determination to stay free and somehow stop what Quentin was doing. He needed to get off the flight deck . . .

The guards were blocking the main doors. The emergency door was at the other side of the deck, and there was a code that had to be entered before it would open. They would shoot him down long before he managed it.

At first, Jake could not think of another way. Then he noticed the inspection panel of the ventilation system. Stepping down to look at Ellie had brought him closer to it. It

25

operated with a single button. And once in the ventilation system, Jake would be able to reach any part of the ship.

He hoped nothing of his idea had shown in his face. Anyway, Quentin was not looking at him. He was watching the main doors, while one hand tapped out an impatient rhythm on the arm of his chair. Mark was gazing at nothing, blank-faced.

The doors swished open again. Two white-uniformed orderlies came on to the deck, with a scared look at the guards, towing an anti-grav stretcher behind them. Quentin pointed them towards Ellie with a flick of one hand. One of the orderlies examined her, and then they lifted her on to the stretcher. The movement did not wake her.

Jake waited. The anti-grav stretcher was awkward when it was loaded and the orderlies were having difficulty in manoeuvring it. As they headed for the doors there would be a moment when they were between Jake and the guards. Jake tensed himself.

The moment came. Jake flung himself across the deck. His hand slapped the button and the panel slid open. He leapt into the dark hole of the ventilation shaft, arms over his head, like a diver cutting water.

Behind him, shouting broke out and he heard feet pounding across the deck.

Chapter Three
Escape Through the Shafts

JAKE SCRABBLED HIS way down the ventilation shaft. Behind him he could still hear shouting, but he could not make out the words. He was terrified. He knew that if a guard fired his laser cannon after him, he would be fried in the shaft, and Quentin's only problem would be how to scrape his remains off the side.

He reached a junction. Panting, he jackknifed his body round the corner and dragged himself clear. A blue glow lit the walls. Twisting his neck to look back, Jake saw laser fire splashing against the shaft wall, but he was safe. He collapsed, gasping for breath. The blue fire died away and left him in darkness.

After a minute he began crawling forward. He wanted to put as much distance as he could between himself and the flight deck. He doubted that Quentin would send a guard after him into the shaft. Those guards were big enough to get stuck. So for the time being he was free, but he was not sure what to do with his freedom.

He tried to remember the diagrams of the *Venture* that he was supposed to be studying. He could reach any part of the ship through the ventilation system, provided he could remember how the shafts were connected. Or he could get hopelessly lost.

He was not sure how long he kept on crawling. He could see nothing and feel nothing except the cold metal of the shaft floor. There was nothing to guide him there.

Then, reaching out, instead of smooth metal, his hand touched nothing.

Thrown off balance, he fell forward. His head and shoulders and grabbing hands met nothing but empty space. The hard edge where the floor stopped pressed against his chest. Dragging himself backwards, shuddering, he realized he had come to one of the vertical shafts that connected the different levels of the ship.

That reminded Jake that the auxiliary control room was one level down from the main flight deck. It might be a good place to make for. Groping carefully, he found a ladder bolted to the wall of the shaft, and lowered himself rung by rung. He was ready to leave this dark maze of metal.

For the first time he asked himself

how he was going to get out. He knew that the inspection panels, like the one he had entered by, opened when you pressed a button on the outside. What he didn't know was how they opened on the inside, or whether they opened at all.

His hands clinging to the ladder were beginning to feel cramped by the time his feet touched the floor at the bottom of the shaft.

For a minute he enjoyed the luxury of standing upright, stretching his cramped muscles. He was on the right level now for auxiliary control. More by luck than clear thinking, he had been moving in roughly the right direction since he left the flight deck.

He needed to find another shaft that would take him further.

Groping with hands outstretched, he found two openings from the vertical shaft. One led back the way he had come. The other went off at an angle. It was not what he wanted, but there was no other choice. Groaning, Jake went down on hands and knees again and fitted himself into the opening. He could not help wondering how many rivets were holding these shafts together.

He began feeling along the wall to find an inspection panel. Shortly his fingers came to a seam in the metal and a shallow, recessed area that was the panel itself. Jake made up his mind.

Much more of these dark passages would send him into gibbering madness. He would try to get out and trust to luck that the control room was not far away.

He crouched in the shaft and began feeling carefully around the edges of the panel. There was no button or any other obvious mechanism to raise it. Also, there was no way for Jake to see what was on the other side.

Eventually he gave up looking for a button, fitted his fingernails into the crack at the bottom of the panel and tugged. To his surprise the panel slid upwards a few millimetres before it stuck.

Light flooded in through the gap,

almost blinding Jake after so long in the dark. Once his eyes were used to it, he lay flat in the shaft and peered out.

Through the crack he could see the ship's teleport terminal. The teleport, looking like a short, grey corridor with a blank wall at the end, was inactive. Usually there was an operator on duty at the bank of controls in front of it, but there was no one there now. The only person in the room was a security guard.

He was facing the door of the terminal, which meant he had his back to Jake. His hands were clasped behind him. He had a stun pistol in the holster at his side, but no other weapon that Jake could see.

Very quietly, trying not to breathe, Jake got another grip on the panel and wrenched it upwards. This time it opened about halfway. The metal edge left weals across Jake's fingers, but by now the gap was wide enough for him to slither out.

He began edging through it as silently as he could, eyes fixed on the security guard. When he was almost out, the guard straightened, began to turn, and saw Jake. He started to shout something, but before he could finish, Jake had propelled himself out of the shaft, grabbed the guard around the legs, and brought him crashing to the deck.

As soon as they fell, the guard was

writing out of Jake's grip, grabbing for his stun pistol. Jake knocked it out of his hand. The pistol went skidding away across the deck. Jake rolled, clutched the pistol, brought it round and fired. A high whining made the air vibrate. The security guard caught the sonic burst full in the chest as he leapt for Jake, then slumped and lay still.

Jake scrambled to his feet and stood looking down at him, feeling slightly sick until he saw that the man was still breathing. He checked the pistol; it was set on 'stun'.

He would have liked to tie up the guard and gag him so he could not give the alarm, but there was nothing to tie him with. Jake was not sure how long he would stay stunned. Better to leave, he thought, get out of the area, so even if the guard reported to Quentin they would not be able to track him down.

He was crossing the room towards the door, still making for auxiliary control, when he brought himself up short. Quentin would be looking for him by now, whether the guard warned him or not. His bright-green cadet shirt was too easily seen. A disguise would be a good idea.

Jake knelt beside the unconscious guard and stripped off the black shirt that showed he was security, pulling it on over his own. From a distance he might pass as a guard himself.

The short pause made him ask

himself what he intended to do when he got to the control room. All the ship's systems could be routed through there, but Jake could hardly run the ship by himself. As a cadet, he did not even know the password that would let him into the ship's computer. And there was no one to help him; anyone who was free now must be in league with Quentin. But if Quentin wasn't there, Jake thought, they might change their minds. He started to feel sick again. He knew what he had to do now. There was no alternative and no one else who would do it for him. If he was to stand any chance of saving the ship, he had to kill Quentin.

Dressed now in the security guard's

shirt, Jake stood up. He took the man's belt as well. Before he put the pistol away he changed the setting from 'stun' to 'kill'.

As he pressed the door button, the ship shuddered violently. The deck bucked under his feet. Jake yelled, staggered and fell. He was sliding across a floor that suddenly wanted to be a wall. As he clawed at the deck plates, another shock wave hit the ship, and all the lights went out.

Chapter Four
Games in the Dark

JAKE CLAWED VAINLY at the deck plates until he slid into the angle between the deck and the wall. He could not see the door, but he knew it was somewhere over his head. He tried crawling

41

upwards, but there was nothing to grip, and he kept slipping back.

Then, gradually, the ship righted itself. The emergency lights blinked on. Jake sat up. He was bruised and winded, but not seriously hurt.

The security guard was still unconscious, sprawled untidily in a corner. Jake left him where he was and went back to the door. It was part-way open, jammed now, but the gap was wide enough for Jake to scramble through.

The corridor outside was empty. Jake drew his pistol again and began moving cautiously in the direction of the control room.

Before he had gone twenty metres, he

was twitching. He kept thinking that he could hear footsteps behind him. He kept expecting to hear someone shout at him and then shoot, or worse — to shoot him without bothering to shout.

He paused with his back against the wall, breathing hard. Trying to stay calm, he called to mind the layout of the *Venture*. On each level, the main corridor ran close to the outside edge with the important areas of the ship on the inside. The teleport terminal was about a quarter of the way round from the control room where Jake wanted to be. He had a long way to go. But he might be able to take a short cut through the middle.

The rec room, he thought.

As soon as the idea came to him, Jake slid round the next corner heading inwards. The recreation room took up a large part of the central section on this level. Jake did not expect anyone to be there. None of the crew who were left would have time to play spaceball, or work out in the gym. Even Quentin would have more on his mind than finding a partner for multidimensional chess.

The entrance to the rec room was an open arch. Jake stepped through warily, glancing from side to side. The tables were empty, the lights out on the games consoles. Some were tipped over, from when the ship had tilted Jake guessed, and the floor was strewn with litter. In the low emergency lighting, the vast sphere of the free-fall spaceball court glimmered like a soap bubble.

Across the rec room, Jake could see the shadowed archway that he wanted to leave by.

"Right. Let's go," he said to himself.

He moved towards it, beginning to relax. This felt better than being out in the corridor where anybody could see him.

Then he froze. He thought he had heard something, a movement, across the rec room to his right. Maybe a footstep?

Everything was quiet. Jake was just managing to convince himself that he had imagined it, when he heard the sound again. Definitely a footstep.

Without thinking, he dived into the cover of the nearest games console. From there he listened again, and finally dared to look out. He could see nothing. He guessed that the intruder might be hidden from him behind the spaceball court.

Have they seen me? he wondered. Are they looking for me?

Using the tables and games consoles for cover, Jake began moving as quickly and quietly as he could, snaking along on hands, knees and elbows, heading for the arch. The pistol in his hand got in the way, but he wanted it ready. At the same time, he tried to keep watch all round him, but he saw no sign of his enemy.

By the time he reached the centre of the room, he had to stop and rest. He lay flat, panting, beside one of the struts that supported the spaceball court. Sweat prickled all over him. Anybody, he thought, would be able to hear his breathing and the pounding of his heart. It was so loud they could probably hear him back on Earth.

As he lay there, Jake made himself listen. His ears tingled with the effort of it. Soon he heard a stir of movement, closer this time. He peered cautiously around the end of the strut, in time to see a dark figure whisk into the shelter of a drinks machine.

Part of Jake wanted to follow and attack and have it over with. The other part told him to get out, fast. Before he could decide, the ship lurched again. The deck tilted. There was the sound of furniture shifting. Somewhere in the distance Jake heard something crash over and tinkle into silence. He grabbed a strut and held on.

With his more urgent worries, Jake had almost forgotten what was happening to the ship. Now he was reminded, he just wanted to lie there and let somebody else sort it all out. He almost envied Mark who still had Quentin to tell him what to do, or Ellie, safely tucked up in Medical.

But as the deck slowly began to

steady itself again, Jake scrambled on to hands and knees and began crawling rapidly towards the way out. Maybe his enemy would still be hanging on to the furniture, too busy to worry about him.

Now there was even more mess on the floor. Jake steered round an overturned chair, a couple of coffee cups, and a half-eaten sandwich. A ball bounced gently past him. Seized by an idea, Jake reached out and grabbed it.

He was kneeling in the space between two tables. The archway was not far away now, but beyond the tables there was no more cover. Jake raised his head, took one look around, and saw nothing. He threw the ball as hard as he could across to the other side of the rec room. As soon as he heard it land, he catapulted himself across the deck towards the arch.

At the same moment, another dark shape shot out of cover. Jake tried to dodge and brought up his pistol, but before he could fire the shape slammed into him. Jake's feet skidded from under him and he crashed to the deck.

All the breath was driven out of him. He writhed under his enemy's weight, trying to free his arm and aim the pistol. Then he heard a voice, loud with outrage.

"Jake Fraser!"

The weight disappeared. Jake rolled over. The pistol snapped up. He just managed to stop himself from pulling the trigger. Standing over him was Ellie.

Chapter Five
Under Attack

JAKE STARED UP at Ellie from where he lay on the deck.

"What do you think you're doing?" he asked, keeping his voice down even though he wanted to shout. "Why'd you attack me like that?"

"Attack you? I didn't attack you," Ellie said. "I just wanted to get to auxiliary control. You attacked me. You were going to shoot me."

She pointed at the pistol, which Jake was still waving around. He sat up and put it in the holster.

"Sorry. I thought you were one of Quentin's thugs," he said, wondering what it was about Ellie that always made him end up apologizing.

"I thought *you* were," she said. "What do you expect if you sneak about like that? I couldn't see you properly in this light." She reached out a hand and hauled Jake to his feet. "And why are you wearing that stupid black shirt?"

Jake looked down at himself. By now the security guard's shirt had collected a good layer of smears and dust from the rec room floor.

"It seemed like a good idea," he said.

Ellie sighed. She looked just as calm as she always did, as if she hadn't just been dodging someone she thought might kill her. Or as if that scene on the flight deck had never happened. Remembering, Jake started to feel awkward.

"Uh – are you all right?" he said.

"Yes, of course I'm all right."

"But you fell – hit your head . . ."

"No, I didn't." Ellie grabbed his arm and began hustling him through the arch and along the corridor. "Let's get under cover, and I'll tell you about it."

Jake could see the sense of that. He managed not to ask any more questions until they had reached the control room. The doors were open; it looked as if that mechanism was jammed as well. Jake asked himself again what was happening to the ship, and what he could be expected to do about it. A heavy, cold feeling started to gather in his stomach.

"I had to get off the flight deck," Ellie started to explain, as soon as they were out of the corridor. "Before Quentin locked us up somewhere – or worse. I hope you didn't think all that sobbing and pleading was real." She fixed Jake with a hard stare.

"Er – no," Jake said weakly.

Ellie let it go.

"I staged the fall," she said. "Just like they teach us to fall in unarmed combat. I was pretty sure that if they took me to Medical I could get away from there. And I did." She took something out of her shirt pocket. "And I brought this with me. If you haven't smashed it, you lunatic. No, it's OK."

She held the object out so Jake could see it – a narrow silvery tube with a seal at one end.

"What's that?" Jake asked.

"Ramitrin-B. If I can jab that into Quentin, it'll put him to sleep for a long, long time."

"And what good do you think that will do?"

Ellie tucked the tube back into her pocket, and fixed the hard glare on Jake again.

"Have you got a better idea?"

"I thought . . . I thought we'd have to kill him."

For a minute they looked at each other. Then Ellie turned away. "That's for later. Right now we have to find out what's gone wrong with the ship."

She strode across the room to the bank of auxiliary controls below the viewing screen. Nothing was activated; the screen itself was a flat, grey square. Everything was still being controlled from the flight deck.

"If I put my mind to it," Ellie said, "I could get this going."

"And Quentin will be down right away to see what's wrong," Jake said.

"Not right away. The lifts aren't working — haven't you noticed? And if we could get those doors closed, we could keep him out for a while at least. Long enough to send off a distress signal."

She bent over and peered at the panels. Jake went to the door and examined its mechanism. In the dim light he could see nothing wrong; he guessed it was the central control that had failed, especially if the lifts were out as well. He fiddled for a while with the button that should have activated the door, but nothing worked — not even thumping it.

"Pity Mark's not here," Ellie said. "He's good with that sort of thing."

"Mark went with Quentin," Jake said. "He gave in."

"Funny," Ellie said, "I wouldn't have expected him to do that."

She shrugged, and went back to poking at the panel. Jake could not help wondering what Mark was doing now. He was surprised to feel vaguely sorry for him. He didn't like Mark, but he knew there would be no future for him with Quentin. He thumped the door again, harder, relieving his feelings, and gave up trying to fix it. He settled for keeping watch on the corridor, his pistol in his hand.

Behind him, various blips and humming sounds were coming from the panel, and exasperated noises from Ellie. Then he heard her grunt of satisfaction.

"That's more like it."

Jake glanced back. Lights were glowing on the central navigation panel.

"Are you going to change course?" he asked.

"What do you think, airhead? I don't know the password. It's communications I want. There."

Another bank of read-outs lit up, flickered, and stayed on.

"Right," Ellie muttered.

She sat in front of the panel and began flicking switches. Jake went back to his watch on the corridor, while Ellie kept up a running commentary from behind him.

"I'm trying to get a status report. We're on emergency life-support — essential areas only. Servo-mechanisms are out. Number three engine down . . . Jake, I don't like this. I think we hit something. Something big."

"You think Quentin needs more parking practice?"

"Or something hit us," Ellie said, as if Jake had not spoken. Her hands danced across the panel. "Let's have the screen," she said. "Then we can — oh!"

Jake stared. As Ellie activated it, the

screen pulsed with blinding light, and then cleared, leaving the familiar backdrop of stars. Only arrowed across it, blocking out the stars, was a ship. It was small; a sleek delta shape, with no identifying markings. It was like nothing Jake had ever seen before, but he knew why he thought it looked dangerous. That design was meant for one thing and one thing only – to hit, and run, fast.

As Jake watched, the strange ship moved in a graceful loop, bringing it closer to the *Venture*. Meanwhile, Ellie was muttering over her read-outs again.

"Defence shields are going down," she said. "Efficiency fifty-six per cent. A couple more blasts and they can fry us."

As she spoke, a dazzling ball of light appeared from the nose of the strange ship, came closer in a curving path until it filled the screen, and vanished. The ship shuddered again.

"Like that," Ellie said.

"Why aren't we firing at them?" Jake asked, agonized.

Almost as if someone was answering the question, a spear of light thrust across the screen, this time coming from the *Venture* itself. It splintered and broke up before it reached the strange ship, as if it had struck an invisible wall.

"Our weapons aren't strong enough."

A new voice joined the conversation. Both cadets spun round. Lieutenant Quentin was standing in the doorway. Jake brought his pistol up, and Ellie's hand moved towards the tube in her pocket, but they both left the movement unfinished. Quentin moved forward into the room.

"We can't break through their shielding," he went on. "The *Venture* is chiefly a courier, remember, not a fighting ship."

He was using his lecturer's voice. He seemed quite cool, unworried by the threat from the two cadets or the danger from outside.

"Then they're going to blast us!" Jake said.

"I think not. They have us in a tractor beam, and I would guess that as soon as our shields are down, they'll board." He glanced from Ellie to Jake and back again. "I'm very much afraid," he said, "that they want us in one piece."

Chapter Six
Enemies on Board

"WHO ARE THEY, sir?" Ellie asked.

She spoke, and clamped her mouth shut, reddening. Jake understood why. That "sir" had slipped out.

Lieutenant Quentin cocked a brow

at the vicious little shape on the screen.

"At a guess, pirates," he said.

"Then you should feel right at home," Jake said. "Are you sure you didn't arrange this?"

For a few seconds, white fury flared up in Quentin's face. Jake had to brace himself not to step back. Then the anger faded. One corner of Quentin's mouth curved in a smile.

"No, Cadet Fraser," he said. "I didn't arrange it."

He stepped past Ellie, took the central seat in front of the panels, and began moving switches.

"What are you doing?" Jake asked.

"Routing control through here. There's damage on the flight deck.

Cadet Carr, you can handle communications. Get off a distress signal. Wide band, random frequency, continuous repeat. If it doesn't do us any good at least High Command will know what's going on in this sector."

Before he had finished speaking, Ellie had turned back to the communications panel and was beginning to key-in the message. Jake kept watching the screen. The pirate craft was closing rapidly.

"What happens now?" he asked.

What happened was another ball of light, arcing out from the pirate craft towards the *Venture*. The ship lurched with the impact; Jake staggered and saved himself from falling by grabbing the edge of the panel.

"Shields, cadet?" Quentin snapped at Ellie.

Ellie swallowed. She was looking sick.

"Eight per cent, sir," she said.

Quentin stood up.

"They can teleport through that," he said. He pulled out his stun pistol. "Cadet Carr, stick with that distress call. Cadet Fraser, come with me."

He led the way out of the control room without even looking to see if Jake was following. Jake exchanged a glance with Ellie, shrugged, and went after him. Part of him still could hardly believe that this was happening, partly he was afraid. But most of all, he felt annoyed that after everything that had

69

happened – even though he knew that Quentin had led a mutiny and spaced the captain and half the crew – even now, Jake found himself automatically obeying.

"I'm not joining you, you know," he said. "I'm not like Mark."

Quentin was moving swiftly down the corridor, back towards the teleport terminal. As Jake spoke, Quentin glanced back. All he said was, "You're improperly dressed, cadet."

Jake's mouth dropped open. His mind grabbed for words, and only came up with, "What?"

"You're wearing the shirt of a rank you've no right to," Quentin said. "And on top of that, it's filthy. If we weren't in this trouble, you would find yourself on report. Again."

"And whose fault is that?" Jake said indignantly.

Quentin did not reply. He had not slackened his rapid pace. Jake gave up.

"What have you done with Mark, anyway?" he asked.

"Cadet Bowman has his orders," Quentin said.

He obviously did not mean to tell Jake what the orders were. Jake lapsed into a disgusted silence. There was no reason for him to worry about what Mark was doing.

As they went on, Jake's senses grew more alert for the sound of footsteps or the soft vibration of stun pistols that might have warned him the pirates were already on board. He heard nothing.

When they came to a cross-passage, Quentin signed to him to stop and peered cautiously round the corner, pistol at the ready. Then he beckoned Jake on.

"I'm guessing they'll board through the terminal," he said. "It's safer. We can't stop them, but what we can do is delay them getting any further into the ship for as long as we can."

"What good will that do?" Jake protested.

"Because —" Quentin began and broke off. "I'll explain later," he said.

If there is a later, Jake thought

silently. Aloud he said, "If there were more of us – if you hadn't spaced all those people – we'd be able to fight!"

Quentin gave him a strange look, a twisted smile, his eyes almost laughing.

"Oh yes," he said. "Believe me, I know that."

"Then why do you –"

Quentin's smile died. "Be quiet, boy," he said irritably. "Or do you want to tell the pirates we're on our way?"

Jake bit back another question. They were close to the teleport terminal by now. A man was standing in the half-open doorway. Jake almost cried out, taking him for a pirate, until he recognized the security guard he had stunned, stripped to the waist and only just starting to recover. So far there was no sign of the pirates.

The guard was hanging on to the door frame, shaking his head to clear it.

"Report, sergeant," Quentin said crisply.

The guard peered at him with bleary eyes.

"Lieutenant . . . sir . . . He stunned me."

"Who?"

The guard waved an arm in Jake's direction.

"Him. And stole my shirt."

"For all the good it did me," Jake muttered.

"And then, he —"

"Very well, sergeant."

Quentin had a brow raised; Jake could have sworn that he was trying not to smile.

"Go and put your head under a tap," he said. "And get dressed. Find yourself a weapon, and then come back. If you can."

The guard sketched a salute and stumbled off down the passage. Quentin looked at Jake, seemed about to say something, and turned back to the teleport terminal. Everything was still quiet.

"If we could close the door . . ." Quentin said.

He pressed the button but the door did not move, and even when both of them tugged together they could not make the panel slide across. There was no time to keep trying. Quentin positioned himself at one side of the gap from where he could see into the room, and placed Jake on the other side. Jake could see nothing but Quentin's tension, his watchfulness. He could hear nothing but his own breathing.

Not sound, but light told him they were on board. The grey light of the teleport, followed by blue laser fire, spilling into the corridor, as if they had come in shooting. Quentin motioned Jake to keep still, and as the first wash of light died he darted forward, snapped off a shot through the half-open door, and slipped back into cover. An answering shot shaved him and spattered harmlessly against the opposite wall.

Jake realized that the pirates would expect more of the crew to be waiting for them. They would never expect a defence of only one officer and a cadet. That alone might keep them penned up for a while at least. Encouraged, not waiting for an order, he thrust an arm round the door frame and shot blind, pulling back to avoid the return fire. He was rewarded by the sound of a curse, and a body slumping to the deck — the first sound their enemies had made. He grinned at Quentin who was looking furious.

"Do you want to lose a hand, boy?" he said.

Before he had finished speaking, the flood of laser light began again, pouring out of the door now in a steady stream, as if the pirates wanted to force their way out under covering fire. Quentin dived under the beams, shot through the door as he hit the deck plates, rolled and came upright beside Jake. He thrust him down the corridor, back to the corner. Blue fire sprayed after them as they skidded into shelter. Jake could see burn marks on Quentin's uniform shirt.

"Are you all right, sir?" Jake asked.

Quentin ignored him. He leant forward, enough to fire down the corridor, and pulled back. Jake did the same. For the first time he saw their enemy. There were five or six of them, dressed in dark-coloured uniforms. Instead of diving for cover they kept moving, coming towards Jake and Quentin. The first two sprayed the passage ahead with laser cannon; the rest followed with stun pistols. Behind them one had fallen and lay in an unmoving heap. Two gone, then, counting the one in the teleport terminal. How many more? Jake wondered.

Crouching low, hoping to confuse them, he got off another shot. The vibrating whine seemed fainter. With a horrible suspicion, Jake checked the charge level on his pistol and drew in his breath sharply as he saw it was nearly drained. Silently he cursed the security guard he had taken it from. Was that any way to maintain a weapon? If Quentin had caught him at it, he would have found himself on report. Jake fought against an insane fit of giggling. What was going to happen now was a lot worse even than one of Quentin's reports.

Without speaking, he held out the pistol and showed Quentin the low charge level. Quentin's brows snapped together and his mouth tightened. He glanced at his own pistol. Jake caught a glimpse of the charge level and saw that it was nearly as low as his own. He could not believe it. Not Quentin! His equipment would always be perfect. But when Quentin fired again Jake could hear that the power was fading. He could not understand it.

The pirates had almost reached their corner.

"What now, sir?" Jake said.

Quentin did not answer. He tried one more shot, but the pistol was drained, the whining noise like a fly buzzing against a window pane. Quentin shrugged, and tossed the useless weapon out into the corridor, where the pirates could see it. He gave Jake one look, almost as if he wanted to say he was sorry, and then raised his hands and stepped out in front of their enemies.

Chapter Seven
Delaying Tactics

JAKE DID NOT know what to do. To run
and hide and stay free to fight again? Or
to keep firing? But his pistol held only
one more shot, at best. In the few
seconds that he dithered, the pirates had

reached the corner and surrounded him and Quentin. A pistol barrel dug into Jake's side.

"Drop it," the pirate said.

Jake hesitated; the barrel dug deeper.

"Do it," Quentin said.

Jake dropped the pistol and one of the pirates kicked it down the passage, well out of reach. They stood bunched together around Jake and Quentin, but they were keeping a lookout in all directions. Jake thought they seemed jumpy. He was not surprised. They could not have been expecting an almost deserted ship.

One of them grabbed Jake, snarling into his face and showing a mouthful of teeth like an old fence, brown and broken. He pawed over Jake with rough hands, frisking him for another weapon. Someone else was doing the same to Quentin. He was a tall man, broad-shouldered, his face heavy and unshaven and threatening. He loomed over the slightly-built Quentin, and pushed him away when he found nothing.

"Where's your captain?" he said.

Quentin did not reply. Almost casually, without any particular anger, the pirate raised his pistol and struck Quentin across the side of the head with the barrel. Quentin dropped to his knees. Blood began to trickle down from his temple.

"Where's your captain?" the pirate repeated.

Quentin still said nothing. Brownteeth grabbed Jake and twisted his arm up behind him. He gasped with the pain.

"Try asking this one," Brownteeth said.

The other — the Chief, Jake called him mentally — was starting to speak when Quentin interrupted.

"Go on, boy," he said. "Tell them everything. Save your miserable skin."

The words were bitter, sneering, and somehow Jake felt they did not sound like Quentin. And Quentin was staring up at him, some kind of urgency in his eyes. Well, Jake thought, an order is an order . . .

"He mutinied and spaced the

captain," he said. "And all the crew who wouldn't follow him."

There was a gleam in Quentin's eyes, as if Jake had just done something clever. Jake could not see what. The Chief looked as if he didn't believe him. His eyes went from Jake to Quentin and back again.

"Spaced the captain?" he repeated.

"Yes," Jake said. "He took the ship. He was going to be a pirate, just like you."

The Chief gave a short laugh, watching Quentin as he got unsteadily to his feet.

"Didn't last long, did it?" he said. "You didn't keep your precious ship for long. Just made it nice and easy for us . . ."

Quentin gave Jake a furious look.

"I didn't hear you complain," he said. "You were happy enough, until this. You went along with it."

That was more than Jake could stand.

"Went along with it!" he yelled. "I was trying to stop you! I wanted to –"

He broke off as Brownteeth wrenched his arm round and pain stabbed him again.

"Shut up," Brownteeth said, "or I'll break it."

Jake shut up. He thought he understood Quentin's plan now, remembering what he said earlier. Delay. Delay by any means. Delay for as long as possible the moment when the pirates took over the ship. What Jake did not understand was why. What help could there possibly be? What difference could a few minutes make? When he could not answer those questions, it was hard to decide whether to go along with Quentin, and whether he wanted to risk being put out of action himself.

While Jake hesitated, the Chief snapped his fingers at another of his troop, a small man with lank hair and a nose like a rat, and set him to guard Quentin. The small pirate grinned.

"Pleasure," he said. He jabbed Quentin with his pistol. "Don't give me no trouble, see?"

Quentin gave him the sort of look

he might have given to a Denebian swamp slug in his salad. Ratnose just went on grinning, while the Chief finished forming up his men. He ordered the last two, the two with the laser cannon, to keep watch behind.

"Let's go," he said. He turned to Quentin. "Where's your flight deck?"

"One level up," Quentin said. "The lifts are out."

Jake had no need to ask himself why Quentin was co-operating now. The answer was obvious. Better to lead the pirates up to the damaged flight deck where there were other crew members, including the goons guarding it with their laser cannon, than let them go anywhere near auxiliary control, where

Ellie was still sending off her distress call.

"Emergency stairs?" the Chief asked.

Quentin jerked his head.

"That way."

The Chief paused, and grinned. He swung round.

"Then we'll go this way."

It hadn't worked. Quentin, grim-faced, was hustled along with Ratnose's pistol in his back, while Brownteeth brought Jake. Jake couldn't think of anything else to do without getting himself shot.

Before they reached auxiliary control, Jake could hear the beeping of the communications panel. Alerted, the Chief strode quickly ahead, checked inside the control room and stood in the doorway with his pistol raised.

As Jake came up to him, he heard him say, "Kill that signal."

Looking in from behind the Chief, Jake could see Ellie, half turned from the panel. Even then she still looked calm, not half as scared as Jake himself felt. She had not obeyed the order. The Chief fired to one side, the sonic charge shrilling past Ellie's head.

"Kill it now," he said.

"Do as he says, cadet," Quentin said.

Ellie did not take her eyes from the Chief. Slowly she reached out and touched a set of switches. The beeping stopped. Some of the lights on the panel went out. The Chief jerked his pistol.

"Move," he said. "Over there."

Ellie left her seat and went to stand beside the wall. Brownteeth shoved Jake up against her and covered the pair of them with his pistol. Ratnose thrust Quentin into the room.

"Now . . ." the Chief said.

He went over to the navigation panel and looked at the controls. Then he turned and trained his weapon carefully on Quentin.

"What's the password?" he asked.

Quentin was silent. Jake knew that the crisis had come. Without the password that would let him into the ship's computer system, the Chief could do nothing. The ship would be just so much expensive junk.

But with it, the ship was his.

Jake's mind spun at the thought of the damage a pirate could do with control of an official courier like the *Venture*. Access to military codes. A brilliant disguise to approach his victims safely. All the information stored in the computers. He could make himself king of this sector of the galaxy. It could be a long time before anyone realized what was happening and stopped him.

The silence lengthened. The Chief's eyes narrowed, and he looked at his men bunched in the doorway.

"You," he said to Brownteeth, pointing to Jake and Ellie, "keep those two out of my hair. You," he said to

Ratnose, "watch the corridor. The rest of you scout ahead."

He waited for his orders to be obeyed, and when the control room was clear he turned back to Quentin. His voice was quiet.

"You're going to answer my next question," he said, "or else I'm going to use this . . ." he hefted his pistol, "to turn your brain into pudding; slowly. You'll be screaming long before I've finished. You *will* tell me, so you might as well tell me now." He smiled, and squinted down the pistol. "What's the password?"

Chapter Eight

A Countdown and a Plan

QUENTIN WAS WHITE, his eyes wide and
dark. He backed away from the Chief's
pistol, until he came up against the
control panel. He gripped the edge of
it, pressing himself back. Jake had once

thought, at the start of all this, that he would like to see Quentin scared, like to see that maddening, cool superiority shattered into tiny bits. Now it was happening, he found he did not like it at all.

Jake expected him to answer. There was nothing to keep quiet for any more. The Chief meant what he said. There was no way that Quentin could keep the ship and live. As for the damage that the Chief could do once he had control, well, Quentin could not possibly care about that. That was just what he himself had meant to do. That was why he had mutinied. And yet Quentin did not answer.

Delay, Jake thought. Was Quentin

still trying to buy time? Buying it at the price of his own torture and death? Jake did not know what he hoped would happen, or what could possibly grab victory out of this miserable defeat. Even if a ship came in answer to the distress call, it would not do Quentin any good. He would be arrested to stand trial, and spend the rest of his life on a prison planet.

"You're being very stupid," the Chief said. Quentin, breathing hard, ignored him. "I'm going to count to five. After that . . ." He paused. "One."

Brownteeth's eyes were riveted on the Chief. He had dismissed Jake and Ellie as not dangerous. He was far more interested in what Quentin would do, or what the Chief would do to him. Jake thought that if he had a weapon, he might be able to surprise him. But he had no weapon.

He felt a sharp dig in his ribs. Ellie, scarcely moving, had managed to jab him with her elbow. When he turned his head to look at her, her eyes were fixed on her shirt pocket. Jake remembered, as if from another century, the hypodermic with the dose of Ramitrin-B, the powerful drug she had meant to use to put Quentin to sleep, that Ellie had stolen from Medical. She had put it in that pocket.

"Two."

When Ellie saw she had his attention, her eyes flickered to the

Chief. Jake had already caught on to her idea but he grabbed back the words he wanted to say. He dared not make a sound. Instead, he let his own eyes flicker to Brownteeth. Ellie gave him a nod, hardly moving at all.

"Three."

Ellie mouthed "Four" at him. Jake returned the tiny nod. Glancing at the door he saw that Ratnose was slouched against the wall, dangling his pistol and chewing something. His face looked vacant. What attention he had was on the passage outside. Ellie's hand was at her shirt pocket, and no one had noticed the movement.

"Four."

Jake sprang at Brownteeth and

brought him down yelling and kicking, grabbing for the hand that held the pistol. Ellie tore the hypodermic out of her pocket and as the Chief swivelled round, she clapped her hand against his shoulder. His pistol went off, angling wildly. Quentin caught the edge of the sonic blast and crumpled to the floor.

Brownteeth twisted to one side, heaved upwards and pinned Jake to the deck. But Jake had hold of his pistol hand by the wrist and forced the barrel back towards him. Brownteeth dared not fire. Dimly Jake saw Ratnose whirl into the doorway, crouching, pistol raised, but he could not fire either. Brownteeth was shielding Jake, and Ellie had darted to one side to put the

Chief between herself and the door.

As if in slow motion, the Chief was swinging his pistol round to train it on Ellie. There was nowhere she could hide. Jake heaved at Brownteeth, but he could not throw him off to free himself and help her. He yelled aloud in fear and frustration.

But as the Chief thrust the pistol into Ellie's stomach, he sagged. His face went slack and his grip gave way. Ellie caught the pistol as he went down, flipped it over, and blasted Ratnose with the full force of the charge. Ratnose stiffened, limbs jerking wildly, and collapsed. Ellie blew across the end of the pistol.

"Works fast, that stuff," she said.

She knelt down beside Jake, who was still locked in his struggle with Brownteeth, and pressed the barrel of the Chief's pistol gently against Brownteeth's ear.

"Drop it," she said.

Brownteeth dropped his own weapon. He looked scared out of what wits he had. Jake snaked out a hand to capture the pistol, and once he had it he let Brownteeth sit up and kept him covered while he and Ellie both looked round and took stock.

The Chief was sleeping peacefully. Just beyond him, Quentin lay face down, twitching now and then. He had not caught enough of the blast to kill him. Jake did not know why he should feel relieved, but he did. In the doorway, Ratnose lay still, either dead or too deeply stunned even to twitch.

Ellie stood up and dusted herself down. She stirred the Chief with her foot, but he did not move.

"Well, that's that," she said.

She went back to the communications panel and started up the distress call again.

"I ought to call Security," she said. "And Medical, for Quentin. But I'm not sure who's still around." She jerked her head towards the pirates. "Or how many more of them we have to deal with."

"Two that I know of," Jake said. "And the two at the teleport terminal were only stunned. They could be starting to come out of it by now. Shall I go and see?"

"No. There's a whole shipful just waiting to board, or had you forgotten? Besides —" Ellie broke off. "Wait," she said. "Listen."

In the distance they could hear the sound of trampling feet and shouting. A lot of people, suddenly spilling into the quiet, almost deserted ship. Pirates, Jake thought. More pirates. A whole shipful of pirates. Panic tore at him. Even now they were properly armed, how could they fight that many?

Then he realized that the sounds were not coming from the teleport terminal, but from the other direction.

They were growing louder. Jake could make out separate voices now, orders being tossed back and forth. Running footsteps, and one of the pirates dashed past the open door, only to be brought down in a burst of sonic fire.

Ellie picked up the Chief's pistol again, slid over to the door and cautiously looked out. Jake could not see what she saw, but he saw her face change. Colour drained out of it. Her mouth widened in a look of complete astonishment. She took a couple of steps back, the weapon in her hand hanging helplessly, as a woman came into the room and looked round.

Behind her others were pressing in. Jake caught a glimpse of Mark, flushed and untidy, a laser cutter in his hand instead of a pistol. But it was hard to drag his eyes away from the first woman, who had come to a halt just inside the control room. A very familiar woman, tall and smiling, her face very faintly surprised.

"Good heavens, you have had a lively time. And what in the world have you done to Lieutenant Quentin?" said Captain Parry.

Chapter Nine
The True Story

"OF COURSE," SAID Captain Parry, pouring coffee, "there was never really a mutiny at all."

Jake gawked, forgetting for a minute the fruit juice and sandwiches on the table in front of him. He was sitting in Captain Parry's private quarters, along with Ellie and Mark and Lieutenant Quentin, who had just arrived after discharging himself from Medical. The lieutenant had a purpling bruise down one side of his face and a dressing on the cut where the Chief had hit him.

Two hours had passed since the scene in the control room. The ship was running normally again, with the engineering techs patching up the damage. The seven pirates who had boarded – all of them, even Ratnose, still alive – were under arrest, although the Chief still did not know it. He was going to have a very nasty shock when he woke up.

Not long after the captain's reappearance, Ellie's distress call had been answered by a very large and very heavily armed battleship, which was now matching speeds with the *Venture*. The pirate ship had surrendered without firing another shot. Presently the battleship would take the pirates, with their ship in tow, back to Earth to stand trial. Jake thought he would be very glad to see the back of them.

He was feeling much more comfortable now. He had found time to shower and put on clean clothes instead of the filthy security shirt. Just as well that Quentin wouldn't have another chance to complain about that.

"What do you mean, there never was

a mutiny?" he asked, and added as an afterthought, "Ma'am."

Quentin wrapped his hands around his mug of coffee, swallowed gratefully, and smiled.

"It was a training exercise," he said.

Jake's mouth dropped open again.

"What?"

"A training exercise," Quentin repeated. "To see how you three would react under stress."

"Then you never spaced all those people?" Ellie said.

Captain Parry brought her own mug of coffee and came to sit down with the rest of them. She gave them her slow smile, and settled herself comfortably.

"Do I look as if I've been spaced?" she said.

"But you told us . . ." Ellie said to Quentin, outraged.

Quentin was looking very white and ill, but his eyes were amused.

"I beg your pardon, I told you no such thing. You jumped to that conclusion. I simply let you believe it."

"And the tech you spaced?" Ellie said suspiciously.

"Oh, him. Yes, rumours do get around, don't they?" Quentin's voice dripped sympathy. "Especially that one, I'm glad to say. I started it myself."

Ellie stared at him.

"But sir . . . did you want us to hate you?" she said.

"It was necessary."

"Why?"

Captain Parry decided to answer that one. Jake munched sandwiches and listened.

"We're not at war," the captain said. "Not at present, though one day we might be. But we can still find ourselves in some pretty dangerous situations, as you yourselves know from experience now. Before cadets can pass out from the Academy, we have to know how they react to danger. If you're threatened – really threatened – will you panic or cave in, or will you try to do something? You three, I may say, came through with flying colours. I shall be attaching a commendation to my report, for all of you."

Jake saw Ellie's eyes brighten, and he thought he must be looking the same. A commendation from their commanding officer at this stage of their career meant a lot. Notice from High Command. Faster promotion. Maybe, in the end, a ship of their own.

If Jake was honest with himself, he knew he and Ellie had both deserved it. But he could not stop himself looking at Mark, and saw him turn slowly red. Jake did not want to say anything because he had gone beyond wanting to score off Mark, but he could not help thinking that Mark had done nothing. He had given in.

Lieutenant Quentin saw the look,

and Mark's embarrassment. Half laughing, half exasperated, he reached out and touched Mark on the shoulder.

"Cadet Bowman here is my failure," he said. "While I was spinning you all that story, he didn't believe a word of it. What gave me away?" he asked Mark. "Was it the medical monitor?"

"Yes, sir." Mark had begun to relax a little. "I'd just given you your life-signs check and everything read out normal. I couldn't believe your stress levels would have stayed down if you'd just spaced the captain and half the crew." Daringly he added, "You're cool, sir, but not that cool."

"Thank you," Quentin said. "How kind."

"It's my pleasure, sir," said Mark, grinning.

Jake stared at him. He would have died before he said anything like that to Quentin! He was sure he would have died afterwards. But Quentin, instead of mincing Mark into tiny pieces, had just grinned back.

"So," he went on, "once the two of you had made your exits, I had to tell Cadet Bowman the truth. And it's just as well I did."

He stopped and drank more coffee. He was starting to look very tired and Captain Parry took up the story again.

"The crew and I, who were

supposed to be dead, were hiding in the cargo bay. Once the attack started, the door mechanisms wouldn't work and we were trapped in there. Lieutenant Quentin sent Bowman down with a laser cutter to get us out."

"I missed all the fun," Mark said. He sounded genuinely sorry.

"Fun!" Ellie said. "It wasn't much fun, I can tell you."

"Exciting, though," Mark said. "Real combat. It's what we're trained for. I . . . I still don't know if I would be any good."

He shrugged uneasily, miles away from the stuck-up Mark Jake had known until now. Jake thought that if he wasn't careful, he might end up liking him.

"Don't blame yourself," Captain Parry said. "To begin with, you used your intelligence instead of just believing what you were told. That's worth something. And after that, you carried out your orders when it wasn't exciting or spectacular, just difficult. If you think that doesn't matter, just remember that the emergency life-support systems don't cover the cargo bay. We were all quietly suffocating in there."

Mark went red again, this time trying to hide how pleased he was. He did deserve the commendation, Jake thought. He wondered whether, in

Mark's place, he could have kept going under that kind of pressure. He might have panicked. Not that he would ever admit it to Mark.

"So that's why you were playing for time!" Jake said to Quentin. "You knew that as soon as Mark let the captain out, we would have enough people to fight. And that's why you wanted me to tell the Chief you'd spaced everybody. So they wouldn't start looking for the people who were missing."

Quentin nodded. He said nothing, but he fingered his dressing and winced. Jake could not help remembering that he had been ready for torture, or death, to win a few extra minutes. He started looking at Quentin

118

with new eyes. It was unexpected, he found, to think of him as a hero, but it wasn't all that difficult.

"You would have let the Chief kill you," he said. "For us – and the rest of the crew."

It felt good, Jake discovered, to have Quentin looking thoroughly embarrassed for once, trying to wave away the praise. Much better than having him look frightened.

"That was nothing," he said, "to what High Command would have done to me if I'd lost the ship."

"They wouldn't have done anything," Captain Parry said. "Because there would have been nothing left when I'd finished with you. No," she said to Jake and Ellie, her face suddenly serious, "I'm very grateful to you for saving him. He can be a pain in the neck, but he has a fine career ahead of him."

By now, Lieutenant Quentin was looking so uncomfortable that Jake felt he had to change the subject.

"And was that why the pistols were drained?" he asked. "Because it was an exercise?"

"Yes, of course," Quentin said. "I didn't actually want you killing anyone." He gave a deep sigh. "Everything came together to weaken the ship. We were very, very unlucky that the attack happened when it did. But we came through it, thanks to you."

Jake felt suddenly brighter. It was true. They had come through. They had won. They were seasoned troopers now. And they each had a commendation to go on their service records. Hungrily, he wolfed down the last of his sandwiches.

"D'you want to go to the rec room?" he asked Ellie and Mark. "I fancy a game of spaceball – loosen up a bit."

Quentin sat up, alert again.

"Rec room?" he said. "Spaceball? Loosen up a bit? You're still on report, lad, and don't you forget it."

Jake stared at him, juice glass forgotten in his hand. He wouldn't dare . . .

"I still want all those rivets counting," Quentin said. He gave Jake a wicked grin. "I reckon you should just about have finished by the time we get back to Earth."